Kidnapped!

Introduction

Volume 1

The so-called Jacobite Revolution in Scotland was an attempt by northern clans to restore a Scottish ruler—a member of the Stuart family—to the throne of Great Britain after three decades of rule by other houses. They felt that King George I, born in Hanover (Germany), had no legitimate claim to the crown. Their revolt in 1714-15 had failed. In 1745 they rebelled again, this time to make their own "Bonnie Prince Charlie" the monarch of the British Isles, but their uprising was harshly put down.

Half a dozen years later, the fires of resentment still smoldered in the Highlands… the hatred of being ruled by a second King George, from far-off London, had not been abated by time… and a sixteen-year-old Scottish lad was about to be swept into the maelstrom of violent events, as related by Robert Louis Stevenson, author of the immortal *Treasure Island…*

Writer: Roy Thomas

Penciler: Mario Gully

Inker: Jason Martin

Colorist: Sotocolor's

A. Crossley

Cover Artist: Gerald Parel

Production: Tom Van Cise

Special Thanks –

Allo, Suter, Nausedas, Ginter

Assistant Editors: Lauren Henry &

Lauren Sankovitch

Editor: Ralph Macchio

Editor in Chief: Joe Quesada

Publisher: Dan Buckley

Spotlight

MARVEL®

VISIT US AT
www.abdopublishing.com

Reinforced library bound edition published in 2011 by Spotlight, a division of the ABDO Group, 8000 West 78th Street, Edina, Minnesota 55439. Spotlight produces high-quality reinforced library bound editions for schools and libraries. Published by agreement with Marvel Characters, Inc.

Printed in the United States of America, Melrose Park, Illinois.
042010
092010
This book contains at least 10% recycled material.

Library of Congress Cataloging-in-Publication Data

Thomas, Roy, 1940-
  Kidnapped! / adapted from the novel by Robert Louis Stevenson ; adapted by: Roy Thomas ; illustrated by: Mario Gully. -- Reinforced library bound ed.
       p. cm.
  "Marvel."
  Summary: Retells, in comic book format, Robert Louis Stevenson's tale of sixteen-year-old David Balfour who, after being kidnapped by his villainous uncle, escapes and becomes involved in the struggle of the Scottish highlanders against English rule.
   ISBN 978-1-59961-781-7 (vol. 1) -- ISBN 978-1-59961-782-4 (vol. 2) -- ISBN 978-1-59961-783-1 (vol. 3) -- ISBN 978-1-59961-784-8 (vol. 4) -- ISBN 978-1-59961-785-5 (vol. 5)
  1. Scotland--History--18th century--Juvenile fiction. 2. Graphic novels. [1. Graphic novels. 2. Scotland--History--18th century--Fiction. 3. Adventure and adventurers--Fiction.] I. Gully, Mario. II. Stevenson, Robert Louis, 1850-1894. Kidnapped. III. Title.
  PZ7.7.T518Kid 2010
  741.5'973--dc22
                                        2009052844

All Spotlight books have reinforced library bindings and
are manufactured in the United States of America.

When your father began to sicken, your mother being gone, he gave me a letter for you, which he said was your inheritance.

He charged me to start you off to the house of Shaws, near Cramond.

"This is the place I came from," he said...

..."and it's where it befits that my boy should return."

What had my poor father to do with the house of Shaws?

The name of that family is the name you bear--"Balfour of Shaws."

An ancient, reputable, if now decayed house...and your father was a man of learning and a teacher of school.

Mr. Campbell, and if you were in my shoes, would you go?

Of a surety, lad. It's near by Edinburgh, but two days of walk.

As for the house's laird*-- remember, it's a pleasure to obey a laird.

I'll promise to try to make it so.

Mrs. Campbell and I want you to have this Bible...

...with a little money for your father's books, which I have bought.

I, for my part, was overjoyed to get away out of that quiet countryside...

...and go to a great, busy house, among respected gentlefolk of my own blood.

*Scotish dialect for "Lord."

"And now come away to your bed."

"I'm just as glad I let you in."

To my surprise, he lit no lamp or candle as he led me up a flight of stairs...

"Here is your room."

"But—I can see nothing. May I have a light to go to bed with?"

"Hoot-toot! There's a fine moon."

"Lights in a house is a thing I don't agree with. I'm that feared of fires."

"Good night to ye, Davie, my man."

I heard him lock me in from outside.

I did not know whether to laugh or cry.

The darkened room was as cold as a well...

...and the bed, when I found my way to it, as damp as a peat rag.

But I caught up my bundle and my plaid...

...and, lying down upon the floor, I fell speedily asleep.

With the first peep of day, I found myself in what must have been a pleasant chamber ten years ago...or perhaps twenty.

So many of the windowpanes were broken that I believe my uncle must at some time have stood a siege from his indignant neighbors...

...perhaps with Jennet Clouston at their head.

Being cold, I knocked and shouted...till my jailer came and let me out.

The kitchen table is laid with a bowl of porridge and a measure of beer.

I'll deny you nothing in reason.

Your mother, too, is dead?

Yes.

Ay, she was a bonnie lassie.

While you're here, I'll ask you to keep your tongue within your teeth.

No letters, no kind of word to friends back in Essendean-- or else there's my door.

Still, I've a great notion of the family, and I mean to do the right by you.

I'm thinking to myself of what's the best thing to put you to--

--whether the law, or the ministry...or maybe the army.

Later, he let me go into a room next to the kitchen, where I found a great number of books, both Latin and English.

I took great pleasure in them all the afternoon.

To
My brother
Ebenezer
on his fifth
birthday

...at puzzled me was that, my father must have been e younger brother, not to ve inherited this house...

...he either made some strange error...

...or he must have written, before he himself was yet five, a manly hand of writing.

Uncle Ebenezer... was my father very quick at his book?

Alexander? Why, I could read as soon as he could!

Why do ye ask that?

Take your hand from my jacket, uncle!

Ye shouldn't speak to me about your father.

He was all the brother that ever I had.

I recalled a ballad of a poor lad who was a rightful heir...

...and a wicked kinsman that tried to keep him from his own.

It had fallen blacker than ever, and I was glad to feel along the wall...

...till I came to the door at the far end of the unfinished wing.

"Keep to the wall! There's no banisters...

"...but the stairs are grand under foot."

NOK NOK

I'll see who 'tis...

It was a half-grown boy in sea clothes...

...who, on seeing us, began to dance some steps of the sea hornpipe.

I've brought a letter from the Cap'n to Mr. Bellflower...

And I say, mates... I'm mortal hungry!

Come in and have a bite, if I go empty for it.

It's from "Captain Elias Hoseason"--who says he's sent his cabin boy to inform you that he's having trouble with a "Mr. Rankeillor."

Davie, I've a venture with this Hoseason, the captain of a trading brig, the Covenant.

If you and me was to walk over with this lad, I could see the Captain...

...and jog on to the lawyer, Mr. Rankeillor's. Rankeillor knew your father.

Yes, I wanted to see that lawyer...

...and a nearer view of the sea and ships.

Very well. Let us go to the Ferry.

NEXT:
I GO
TO SEA